Learn good manners

with Charles

My cousin Trevor has never said "thank you".

Trevor doesn't know anything about being polite. Whenever I receive something or ask for something, I always use polite words like "thank you" and "please."

Trevor never says
"excuse me".

If I run into someone, even if it's by accident, or if I do something wrong, I always say "excuse me" or "I'm sorry."

Trevor isn't even polite enough
to say "hello!"

When I see an acquaintance or
a friend, I'm always sure to say
"hello" and a polite "good-bye"
when I leave.

Without a second thought, Trevor always elbows his way to the front of the line.

When I see people patiently waiting, I join them at the end of the line. It's just the way things are done where everyone is nice to each other.

That rude Trevor always interrupts.

How disrespectful! I listen to others as they speak; then I reply when they have finished.

Trevor is disgusting; he always speaks with his mouth full of food.

Me, I never speak with my mouth full. I don't speak until after I have swallowed my food. It is definitely more polite.

Trevor never offers his seat
to anyone else.

When I see an elderly person
or a lady who is expecting
a baby, I always offer him
or her my seat.

When Trevor yawns, he leaves
his mouth wide open for all to see.

*I don't think that's very
pleasant. When I yawn
or sneeze, I cover my mouth
with my hand. It is certainly
more civilized.*

When Trevor needs something,
he just grabs it.

My cousin is never
embarrassed. I always ask
before borrowing an item
from someone.

When Trevor eats, he always flops
his elbows on the table.

My cousin has really poor table
manners. I always sit up
straight in my chair, and
I never put my elbows
on the table.

Without ever thinking about it,
Trevor throws trash on the ground.

I always look for a trash can in which to put my trash. I'm not like my cousin; I want to keep our planet clean.

Trevor points his finger at others.

If I have something to say about someone, I describe him or her in as much detail as possible. No matter what, I never point.